FIRE! FIRE!

Hilde Cracks the Case

HAVE YOU READ ALL THE MYSTERIES?

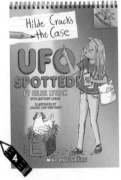

More books coming soon!

scholastic.com/hilde

Hilde Cracks the Case

FIRE! FIRE!

BY HILDE LYSIAK
WITH MATTHEW LYSIAK

ILLUSTRATED BY
JOANNE LEW-VRIETHOFF

BRANCHES

SCHOLASTIC INC.

To my big sister and photographer, Isabel Rose Lysiak,
who may be awesome, even if she sometimes has to get
bossed around by her little sister :)

If you purchased this book without a cover, you should be aware that this
book is stolen property. It was reported as "unsold and destroyed" to the publisher, and neither the
author nor the publisher has received any payment for this "stripped book."

Copyright © 2018 by Hilde Lysiak and Matthew Lysiak
Illustrations copyright © 2018 by Joanne Lew-Vriethoff

Jacket photos © Dreamstime: Kavee Pathomboon, Frbird; _human/Thinkstock.
Hilde's photo courtesy of Isabel Rose Lysiak.

Photos ©: cover spirals and throughout: Kavee Pathomboon/Dreamstime; Hilde's photo: Isabel
Rose Lysiak; back cover paper: Frbird/Dreamstime; back cover tape: _human/Thinkstock; back cover
paper clip: Picsfive/Dreamstime; 88 paper clips and throughout: Fosin2/Thinkstock; 88 pins: Picsfive/
Dreamstime; 88 bottom: Courtesy of Joanne Lew-Vriethoff; 88 background: Leo Lintang/Dreamstime.

All rights reserved. Published by Scholastic Inc., Publishers since 1920.
SCHOLASTIC, BRANCHES, and associated logos are trademarks
and/or registered trademarks of Scholastic Inc.

The publisher does not have any control over and does not assume any
responsibility for author or third-party websites or their content.

No part of this publication may be reproduced, stored in a retrieval system,
or transmitted in any form or by any means, electronic, mechanical, photocopying, recording, or
otherwise, without written permission of the publisher.
For information regarding permission, write to Scholastic Inc.,
Attention: Permissions Department, 557 Broadway, New York, NY 10012.

This book is a work of fiction. Names, characters, places, and incidents are either the product of the
authors' imagination or are used fictitiously, and any resemblance to actual persons, living or dead,
business establishments, events, or locales is entirely coincidental.

Library of Congress Cataloging-in-Publication Data

Names: Lysiak, Hilde, 2006- author. | Lysiak, Matthew, author. | Lew-Vriethoff, Joanne, illustrator.
Title: Fire! fire! / by Hilde Lysiak, with Matthew Lysiak ; illustrated by Joanne Lew-Vriethoff.
Description: First edition. | New York, NY : Branches/Scholastic Inc., 2018. |
Series: Hilde cracks the case ; 3 | Summary: When Nina's antique store burns down, nine-year-old
reporter Hilde and her sister/photographer, Izzy, are determined to investigate the cause for the
Orange Street News—and their main clue is a bird's nest of baby blue jays.
Identifiers: LCCN 2017022639| ISBN 9781338141610 (pbk.) | ISBN 9781338141627 (hardcover)
Subjects: LCSH: Reporters and reporting—Juvenile fiction. | Fires—Juvenile fiction. | Birds—Nests—
Juvenile fiction. | Detective and mystery stories. | CYAC: Mystery and detective stories. | Reporters
and reporting—Fiction. | Fires—Fiction. | Birds—Nests—Fiction. | GSAFD: Mystery fiction. |
LCGFT: Detective and mystery fiction.
Classification: LCC PZ7.1.L97 Fi 2018 | DDC 813.6 [Fic] —dc23
LC record available at https://lccn.loc.gov/2017022639

10 9 8 7 6 5 4 3 2   19 20 21 22

Printed in China 62
First edition, January 2018
Edited by Katie Carella
Book design by Baily Crawford

Table of Contents

Introduction. 1

1: Hot Tip! 3

2: Risky Move 6

3: All Fired Up! 14

4: Fire! Fire! 19

5: Cheep! Cheep! 23

6: Witness 29

7: A Perfect Match? 34

8: Little Survivors 40

9: Fire Station 46

10: Pet Growl! 52

11: Sudden Spark 58

12: One Wild Ride! 68

13: Crack in the Door 74

14: A Surprise from Above 79

Selinsgrove

Eighth Street

Mill Street

Orange Street

Market Street

Pine Street

Front Street

Susquehanna River

IMPORTANT PLACES

1	Nina's Antique Store	2	Fire station
3	Mrs. Brown's house	4	Police station
5	Kind Kat Café	☆	Hilde's house

Introduction

Hi! My name is Hilde. (It rhymes with *build-y*!) I may be only nine years old, but I'm a serious reporter.

I learned all about newspapers from my dad. He used to be a reporter in New York City! I loved going with him to the scene of the crime. Each story was a puzzle. To put the pieces together, we had to answer six questions: Who? What? When? Where? Why? How? Then we'd solve the mystery!

I knew right away I wanted to be a reporter. But I also knew that no big newspaper was going to hire a kid. Did I let that stop me? Not a chance! That's why I created a paper for my hometown: the *Orange Street News.*

Now all I needed were stories that would make people want to read my paper. I wasn't going to find those sitting at home! Being a reporter means going out and hunting down the news. And there's no telling where a story will take me . . .

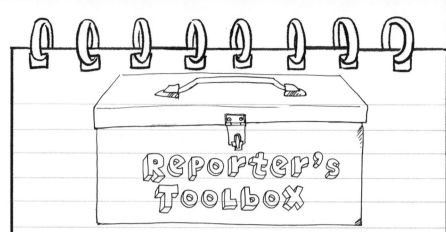

Active Scene: a place where emergency workers are still doing their jobs

Confession: when someone finally admits what he or she did

Evidence: something that helps prove if a theory is true

Hook: something interesting that draws the reader into a story

Investigate: to dig deeper into a story

Notepad: where a reporter keeps clues, quotes, and important notes

Source: a person who gives information to a reporter

Theory: an idea that hasn't been proven yet

Tip: a new bit of information about a story

Witness: a person who sees something happen

1 Hot Tip!

WROOR! *WROOR!*

"Sirens!" my older sister, Izzy, screamed.

The sound of sirens meant only one thing to a reporter — breaking news. I jumped on my bike.

Red and white flashing lights whirled past in a blur.

A gust of wind hit us.
"I smell smoke!" I said.

The fire engine and the smoke told me *what* was happening: a fire. But I needed a lot more answers if I wanted to have a story fit for the *Orange Street News*.

Who? What? When? Where? Why? How?

Izzy and I pedaled as fast as we could, following the truck down Orange Street until we got to the corner of Mill Street.

"It went that way," I said, pointing up the street. We both looked left — and what we saw next was shocking!

2 Risky Move

A large cloud of smoke was rising up into the sky!

"The fire's only a block away!" I said.

"Oh, no! Nina's Antique Store!" Izzy said.

We raced closer. The fire truck was blocking the street. We could see Archie the fire dog near it. He was a friendly Dalmatian that lived at the fire station.

Yellow tape stretched across Mill Street. A reporter knows what that means: Don't cross the line!

We rode up to the tape, dropping our bikes on the sidewalk.

I squinted and cupped my hand on my forehead to block the bright sunlight. I could see red flames shooting through the store's top window, near the roof.

Firefighters were spraying water on the fire.

"At least Nina's safe," said Izzy. "I see her over there."

"But she loved her store. She must be so upset," I said.

I never actually bought anything from Nina's store, but it was a super fun place to visit. Nina loved talking about her antiques, and she had a story about each one.

Nina also had a pet parakeet named Boots. He had bright white feathers and could repeat words he heard. Nina often let him perch on her shoulder.

"I hope Boots is okay," I said to Izzy, trying to hide the worry in my voice.

"I can't believe this is happening," said Izzy. "We just interviewed Nina last week for that story about her new lights."

Nina had recently purchased a string of special lights — shaped like owls — that hung all around the outside of her store. Nina said squirrels had been digging holes in her roof. She hoped these lights might scare them away, since squirrels are afraid of owls. That gave me a great hook for my news story: Local woman tries to outsmart pesky squirrels! And Izzy's picture of the lights looked cool.

Local Woman Outsmarts Squirrels

Now Nina's lights — and the rest of her store — were destroyed.

Part of me wanted to cry, but tears weren't going to help. Not when I needed answers! I pulled out my notepad.

WHAT: A fire

WHERE: Nina's Antique Store

Izzy pulled out her camera. *Click!*

"Keep taking pictures while I try to find a witness," I said.

I looked across the street. Mill Street neighbors were staring at the fire — witnesses! But they were on the other side of the yellow tape. I sighed. I would have to go *all the way* around the block. I didn't have time! This was breaking news!

I looked around. No one was watching. Besides, the fire was basically out. *I'm sure it would be okay if I just quickly sneaked across . . .*

I dipped under the tape.

Just then, I felt a gust of wind. The next thing I knew, a thick cloud of smoke had surrounded me.

I began to cough. The smoke made my eyes water and burn. I couldn't see!

I stumbled backward.

Suddenly, two large hands lifted me up into the air!

3 **All Fired Up!**

My feet thudded on the ground. I was safely out of that dark cloud, but who had grabbed me?

I wiped smoky tears from my eyes and saw Chief Vince. He did not look happy!

Chief Vince was in charge of the Selinsgrove Fire Department. He didn't like being interviewed by reporters, but he would always do his best to help if I had a question. He was what I call a *so-so* source.

The fire chief wrinkled his nose. That meant I was in trouble.

"Hilde, I know *you* know what yellow tape means," he said. "It's there to keep you safe."

I looked down. I felt embarrassed. I had only been trying to save time, but breaking the rules had clearly put me in danger. And Chief Vince seemed mad. I didn't want to lose a source over this!

The fire chief looked me in the eye. "Fires are dangerous," he continued. "You could have gotten hurt. What were you thinking, Hilde?"

"I'm sorry," I said. "I just wanted to interview those witnesses over there. I didn't think —" I knew better than to make excuses. I cut myself off. "It won't happen again."

"It'd better not," he said.

Then Chief Vince smiled ever so slightly.

Phew! He's not that mad!

I pulled out my notepad.

"While you're here, any chance I could ask you a few questions?" I asked.

His smile disappeared.

"This isn't a good time, Hilde. The fire is not quite out yet so this is still an active scene." Chief Vince rushed away.

I was about to start my trip around the block when Izzy ran up to me.

"I got great pictures," she said. "Did you find witnesses?"

"Well, yes and no," I sputtered.

Izzy's eyebrows crinkled in the middle. "Were you crying? Your eyes are all red."

"Of course I wasn't crying," I said, rolling my eyes. "It's a long story."

I checked my phone: 9:30 a.m. I didn't need to post my news story until 6 p.m., so I had plenty of time to get the scoop. But Izzy and I had to be home by noon for a cookout.

"Let's take a ride around the block," I said, pulling Izzy toward our bikes. "I need to interview those witnesses."

But then we heard someone crying.

"Who's crying?" Izzy asked.

"I'm not sure," I said. "Let's find out."

4 Fire! Fire!

We followed the sound of crying to a tree.

It was Nina! Her parakeet, Boots, was perched on her shoulder. I was glad to see he was safe, but sad to see Nina was so upset.

We leaned our bikes against a telephone pole. I kept my notepad in my pocket. A reporter knows to treat an upset witness with care.

Izzy and I sat down beside Nina.

"I'm so sorry about your shop," I said.

"Me too, Nina," added Izzy.

"Thank you, girls," Nina said. "I'm just glad no one was hurt in the fire."

"Fire! Fire!" Boots repeated.

We all chuckled. Even Nina. It felt good to laugh after something so sad had happened.

"Would you be able to tell us what happened?" I asked.

Izzy gave me a look and added, "But we understand if it's not a good time."

"It's okay," said Nina. "But I don't *know* what happened."

"Anything you can remember might help," I said as I pulled out my notepad.

Nina rubbed her chin. "Well, I was at home when I got a call from Chief Vince that there was a fire at my store. I got here as quickly as I could. But since the building was so old and made of wood, the fire spread fast."

"What time did you receive the call?" I asked.

"Hmmm. Around nine this morning," said Nina.

Izzy turned to me. "That was about the same time we first heard the sirens."

I nodded.

"Anything else you might remember?" I asked.

"No. Sorry, girls," Nina said.

"That's okay," I said as Izzy and I stood up.
"Thank you. And we are really sorry. We know
how much you loved your antiques."

"Oh, my antiques are okay," Nina replied.

Izzy turned to me.

"How can Nina's antiques be okay if her store
burned down?" she whispered. "That doesn't
make sense . . ."

5 Cheep! Cheep!

"Nina, are you sure your antiques weren't destroyed in the fire?" I asked.

"Luckily, I had moved them out of my store yesterday," Nina explained. "I'd wanted to make room for Mrs. Brown to sell her candles."

"Candles?" I said, taking notes. Then I remembered. "The Pet Prowl is today!"

The Selinsgrove Pet Prowl is a parade where dogs, cats, and other pets wear costumes and march down Market Street. After the parade, the animals all get to enjoy treats like biscuits for dogs, nip for cats, and even seeds for the birds. A judge awards a thousand dollars to the pet with the best costume.

"Yes, that's today," said Nina. "And Mrs. Brown always makes animal-shaped candles that she sells before the parade. Everyone loves to collect her candles. Last year, she made colorful bird-shaped candles."

Izzy nodded. "I remember — Mom and Dad bought one."

"They really are beautiful," Nina said. But then she smiled sadly. "Mrs. Brown had set up her candles last night so she'd be ready to sell them first thing today. It sounds like she was at my store bright and early. Thankfully, she wasn't hurt in the fire."

"Have you spoken to Mrs. Brown today?" I asked.

"No, she was still being interviewed by the police," said Nina.

"Cheep! Cheep!" said Boots.

Izzy and I laughed.

"I've never heard Boots make that sound before," I said.

"You have good ears!" said Nina. "Blue jays have been making *cheep* sounds outside my store all week. And you know how Boots likes to repeat everything he hears."

We smiled and picked up our bikes.

"By the way," Nina added. "Could you send me those pictures you took last week — the ones from your story about my owl lights? I'd like to remember my store the way it was before the fire."

"Of course!" Izzy said.

"Thanks again for your help, Nina," I said.

I looked at my notes.

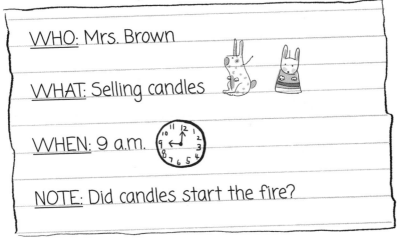

WHO: Mrs. Brown

WHAT: Selling candles

WHEN: 9 a.m.

NOTE: Did candles start the fire?

I still needed a lot more answers if I was going to get my story.

My next question — *how*? How did this fire start?

I turned to Izzy. "We need to talk to Mrs. Brown. It sounds like she was in the store when the fire started. She could have some answers!" I said.

"Yes," Izzy agreed. "Let's head back to the scene of the fire!"

6 Witness

We set our bikes down on the sidewalk. Smoke was still rising from the building, but the fire was completely out now.

Izzy spotted Mrs. Brown talking to Officer Wentworth.

We walked up just as the police officer was walking away.

Mrs. Brown's eyes were red.

Izzy kept her camera at her side.

"Hi, Mrs. Brown," Izzy said.

"Hi, girls," she answered. "I suppose our town's crime reporter has some questions for me, too."

"If that's okay?" I asked.

Mrs. Brown sniffled, then nodded.

I took out my notepad.

"Thank you," I said. "Could you please tell us what happened this morning?"

"I feel terrible about the fire," said Mrs. Brown. "Nina was kind enough to let me use her store to sell my candles."

She bit her lip. I could tell it was difficult for her to talk about what happened.

After a short pause, Mrs. Brown continued. "Well, I had everything set up by eight forty-five a.m. and the store was full of my bunny-eared candles. Then suddenly, I smelled smoke. But I couldn't tell where it was coming from. I started coughing and ran outside to call nine-one-one. The fire truck pulled up a couple minutes later, but it was too late. The fire had spread quickly."

I wrote everything down.

"Were candles lit at the time of the fire?" I asked.

"Yes," answered Mrs. Brown. She swallowed hard. "I had lit some so people would smell their sweet scents when they walked in. One of them must have somehow set the store on fire." She broke down in tears. "Oh, it was all my fault! I just know it. I ruined Nina's store!"

I wanted to ask more questions, but I knew this wasn't a good time.

"Thank you for talking to us," I said.

"Well, I guess this case is closed," Izzy said as we walked away. "We have a confession: Mrs. Brown just said her candles set the fire."

"Not so fast," I said. "Mrs. Brown *thinks* her candles started the fire. That's her theory. But a theory isn't a fact."

I felt something wet splatter on my shoulder. Izzy pointed at me and started laughing.

"What was that?!" I cried.

7 A Perfect Match?

"**H**ilde, a bird pooped on your shoulder!" Izzy cried, still laughing.

I felt my face turn red. "Gross!" I said.

Suddenly, Izzy gasped. "Oh, no."

"What's wrong?" I asked.

"It's the Mean-agers!" she said. "They're coming our way!"

The Mean-agers are a group of Orange Street teenagers known for their rotten attitudes. Three of them — Maddy, Donnie, and Leon — strutted over.

As soon as they saw the white patch on my shoulder, they started laughing.

"It looks like we aren't the only ones who think you make a better toilet than a reporter," said Maddy.

Donnie gave Maddy a high five.

Leon was laughing so hard he bent over. Things spilled out of his jacket pocket. I watched as he picked up a white comb, a dollar bill, and a pack of matches.

I wrote the items down in my notepad.

"Real funny," said Izzy. "Why don't you three just make like a tree and leave?"

The Mean-agers stepped closer to us.

Then we heard an ice-cream truck nearby.

"Ice cream!" yelled Donnie.

They took off running.

We picked up our bikes.

I found a leaf and used it to wipe off the mess on my shirt.

I looked at Izzy.

"'Make like a tree and leave?'" I said. "That was the best you could do?"

Izzy narrowed her eyes. "Yeah, well at least I said something. You just scribbled in your notepad," she said. "Anyway, I wish I had gotten a picture of the bird poop on your shoulder. Talk about front-page news!"

I couldn't help it. I started laughing — and Izzy did, too.

"Okay," I said. "Now we need to get back to work. Can you guess what I was scribbling?"

"The matches?" Izzy replied.

I nodded. "Maybe Leon started the fire and —"

"Look!" cried Izzy. Chief Vince was taking down the yellow tape. "Let's go get a closer look!"

We walked over.

The building was still standing, but there were scorched boards, and puddles all over the sidewalk. We searched for clues as to what had caused the fire.

Izzy took pictures. She even got a pic of Nina's owl-shaped lights — or what was left of them.

Suddenly, we heard a sound.

Cheep! Cheep!

We looked around.

Cheep! Cheep!

"It's coming from under there," I said, pointing. "This gutter must have fallen during the fire."

I stepped toward it.

"Careful, Hilde!" Izzy warned. "The metal could be hot! And we don't know what's under there!"

8 Little Survivors

I carefully lifted the gutter with my foot — and uncovered two baby blue jays!

Cheep! Cheep!

"Awww! They're so cute!" Izzy said.

"Should we pick them up?" I asked.

"Hmm . . . I'm not sure," Izzy answered. "Maybe we should ask Officer Pam."

Officer Pam is a wildlife officer whose job is to help animals. She also judges the Pet Prowl. The *Orange Street News* worked with her once before — when a bear was loose in Selinsgrove.

"That's a great idea!" I said.

I called Officer Pam. She answered right away and I told her what we'd found.

"I'll be right over," she said.

While we waited, Izzy took more pictures and I kept an eye on the baby birds.

Soon, Officer Pam's van pulled up.

I waved her over. She was holding a clear container and wearing special gloves.

"Good thing you called. These little chicks look like they are having a rough time," she said.

Officer Pam carefully scooped up the chicks. They chirped playfully as she placed them in the container.

I pulled out my notepad.

"Oh, I see," Officer Pam said, smiling. "Is this your next big story?"

"A reporter is only as good as her next story," I said.

"We are investigating the fire," Izzy added.

"So how did a bird's nest end up underneath this gutter?" I asked Officer Pam.

"Birds often build nests in gutters because the tunnel-like shape helps keep their chicks safe from cold or wind. It also keeps them hidden from hungry critters," Officer Pam explained. She glanced at the remains of the fire. "Unfortunately, a gutter can't keep birds safe from everything."

"What do you mean?" I asked.

"Well, it's a miracle these two little chicks survived the fire. I'm guessing their parents either weren't at home when the fire broke out or they weren't so lucky."

Izzy shook her head. "I bet those chicks are chirping because they miss their mom and dad."

Officer Pam nodded her head sadly. "Now I've got to get these chicks to the wildlife center so they can be checked out."

Officer Pam climbed back in her van. "Good luck with your story, girls. I'll see you at the parade!" she called out before driving off.

Wildlife I

"I don't think we're going to find anything else here," Izzy said. "Besides, I got pictures of everything. We can always review them for clues later."

We picked up our bikes.

"I wish we knew how this fire started," I said. "We know Mrs. Brown was in Nina's store — with her candles lit — before it broke out. But we need proof that it was her candles that actually lit the fire that burned down the building."

I had an idea.

"Let's go to the fire station," I said. "Maybe Chief Vince has more information by now."

Izzy glanced at her phone. "We better hurry. It's eleven thirty!"

We were riding down Mill Street when we heard a voice screeching, "Fire! Fire!"

9 Fire Station

I stopped pedaling.

"Another fire?" I asked.

"No, silly," said Izzy. "Look up!"

I looked up — and saw Nina's parakeet, Boots!
He was flying above us.

Boots looked different now than he did earlier. His pure white feathers were dotted black.

"Fire! Fire!" he screeched again, then flew out of view.

"That's strange," I said. "I've never seen Boots apart from Nina before. And what were those black splotches?"

"Yeah," said Izzy. "Boots must have somehow gotten loose. We better tell Nina right away."

"We won't have to go far," I said. "Look!"

"Boots! Boots!" Nina called out. She was running down the block!

She stopped when she saw us.

"Have you seen Boots?" she asked. She was out of breath. "He chased after a flock of blue jays."

"He just flew that way," said Izzy, pointing toward Front Street.

"But Nina," I added, "why is Boots covered in black dots?"

"Oh, that silly bird was poking his beak around in the ashes at my store. It was like he was looking for something," she said, shaking her head. "I just lost my store . . . I can't lose my pet today, too!"

Nina sprinted down the street.

"Let's get to the fire station," I said to Izzy. "We need answers."

Izzy and I biked to the corner of Front Street. We parked in front of the station.

Chief Vince was outside with Archie.

"Hello, girls," he said as we walked up.

Archie rolled over so his belly was in the air. Izzy knelt down to pet him.

I pulled out my notepad.

"Hi, Chief Vince," I said. "I was hoping you could share any information you might have about what started the fire at Nina's store."

"We are still investigating the cause of the fire," the chief said. "But there is one thing I can tell you: The fire started on the right side of the roof, near the gutter."

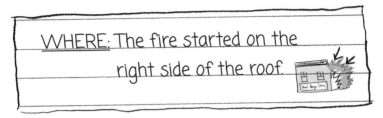

WHERE: The fire started on the right side of the roof.

"Thanks for the tip," I said.

"No problem," he said. "Stay safe!"

Izzy turned to me. "The roof? Mrs. Brown said she lit her candles *inside* the store. And her candles were on the first floor."

"That means her candles couldn't have started the fire!" I said. "But if they didn't start the fire, then what did?"

"I don't know," Izzy said. "And I'm not sure where else we can look for answers."

I glanced at my phone. 11:45 a.m.

"We need to be home in fifteen minutes anyway," I said. "So let's head there for now."

We hopped on our bikes and pedaled back up Mill Street. We kept our heads down as we pushed hard on our pedals. Then —

Izzy and I slammed on our brakes!

10 Pet Growl!

A group of people was standing in the middle of the street.

"Why is everyone in the road?" Izzy asked me.

I was about to say I had no idea, when I heard a very loud bark —

GRRUUUUUFFFFFF!!!

A lion ran up to me! Well, not a *real* lion. It was actually a tiny, scruffy-haired black dog dressed like a lion. It was Zeus — and his owner, Mr. Macintosh.

Izzy and I laughed. Zeus looked adorable in his costume!

"It must be time for the Pet Prowl," I said as I leaned down to pet Zeus.

"Almost," said Mr. Macintosh. "The parade starts at two. The judges are going to give out the prize for the best costume after that. And of course, all the pets are excited for their special treats."

I could see dog treats, cat nip, and a bird feeder set up near the end of Market Street.

I looked at my phone. 11:50 a.m.

"Why are you all here so early?" I asked.

"Everyone who wants to participate was supposed to meet at the corner of Market and Mill Streets at noon to register," said Mr. Macintosh.

"Oh, okay," I said.

Just then, our neighbor Sue elbowed past Mr. Macintosh.

"We have a big problem," she announced to the crowd. "Mrs. Brown isn't coming, so there's no one here to register the pets!"

"Oh, no!" said Glenn, who owns the Kind Kat Café and has three cats. "Mrs. Brown has all the registration information. She organizes everything for the Pet Prowl. We can't have the Pet Prowl without her!"

"We saw Mrs. Brown earlier today," said Izzy. "Why isn't she coming?"

Mrs. Taggert, another one of our neighbors, spoke up. "I just got back from Mrs. Brown's house. She feels *so* bad about causing the fire at Nina's store that she has locked herself in her house. She is refusing to come out."

Mr. Macintosh stepped forward. "Let's all come back at two," he said. "But if Mrs. Brown isn't here by then, we will have to cancel everything. Without Mrs. Brown, there is no Pet Prowl."

Everyone began walking away.

Izzy and I looked at each other.

"This is terrible!" Izzy said.

"The fire wasn't even her fault!" I added. "We have to go talk to her."

"You're right," Izzy said, "but first we need to get home for the cookout."

"Good point! No one will be back here until two anyway, so it's the perfect time for a lunch break," I said. "Hey, I wonder what our headline should be for this story . . ."

"Hurry, Hilde!" Izzy said, jumping on her bike. "If we don't make it home in two minutes, Dad will have his own headline for us: GROUNDED!"

11 Sudden Spark

Izzy and I ran into the backyard at noon on the dot. *Phew!*

Dad was getting ready to start the fire in the pit. He didn't seem to notice the time — or that we were out of breath.

"Hey, girls," he called out.

"Hi, Dad!" we yelled back.

Our little sisters — Georgie and Juliet — were playing nearby. They were hunting for something in the grass.

"Dad, what are Georgie and Juliet looking for?" I asked.

"Kindling," Dad replied.

"What's kindling?" asked Izzy.

Dad picked up Georgie's collection of sticks. "Kindling is small sticks or twigs used to start a fire."

"Why can't you just use matches?" I asked.

"Matches can be used to light the kindling," Dad explained. "But they wouldn't create enough of a flame on their own. We need the lit kindling to catch the bigger logs on fire."

Mom set a pitcher of lemonade down on the picnic table.

"Why don't you girls go wash your hands?" she said.

We ran inside. By the time we came back out, Dad had the fire going.

Izzy, Georgie, and I took turns holding our hot dogs in the fire until they were crispy. Mom helped Juliet with hers.

After we finished eating, I checked my phone. It was already 1 p.m.!

"Izzy, the Pet Prowl begins in one hour," I said. "We need to get to Mrs. Brown's house!"

Izzy scratched her head. "Let's read over our notes first — just to make sure we're right about everything before we see her."

"Good idea." A reporter always double-checks her facts.

Mom excused us from the table, then we ran up to my bedroom.

Izzy and I sat side by side on my bed. She took out her laptop. I opened my notepad.

I reread my notes . . .

WHAT?

❋ A fire!

WHERE?

❋ Fire started on right side of roof.

WHEN?

❋ This morning around 9 a.m.

WHO? – WHO CAUSED THE FIRE??

❋ Mrs. Brown (She was in the store when the fire started.)

❋ Leon (Matches fell out of his pocket!)

❋ Someone else??

WHY?

❋ Need to investigate more to find the answer to this question!

HOW?

* Sweet-scented bunny-eared candles?

BUT... The candles were on the first floor. The fire started near the roof, so it could NOT have been caused by the candles...

Boots chased after a flock of blue jays.

Blue jays made a nest in the store's gutter.

"We need to figure out how the fire started *on the roof*," I said.

"I feel like we are hitting a dead end," said Izzy.

"What about Leon?" I asked.

"The Mean-agers could have something to do with the fire," replied Izzy, "but we didn't find any other evidence pointing to them."

"That's true . . ." I said.

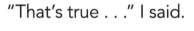

Izzy pulled the pictures up on her laptop.

"Hey, don't forget to send Nina those pics from before the fire," I said.

"Oh, yeah," Izzy said. "I'll do that now."

A picture of Nina's store popped up onscreen. The store looked so colorful and welcoming before the fire. Looking at it made me feel sad again.

"Hey, look," said Izzy.

"What?" I said.

"Look near the gutter on the right side — behind this owl-shaped light." She pointed. "See those twigs sticking out? I bet that's the blue jays' nest — where those cute little chicks lived. It actually looks like there might be more than one nest . . ."

Izzy zoomed in.

There wasn't just one nest! There were *three*! And they were all nestled between the wooden wall and Nina's new, owl-shaped lights.

"That's it!" I cried.

"Wait," she said. "What?"

"You're a genius, Izzy!" I yelled. "I'll explain later. Print out that picture, grab your magnifying glass, and let's go! We need to show this to Chief Vince right away!"

"What about Mrs. Brown?" asked Izzy.

"We'll head to her house *after* we talk to the chief," I said. "Come on!"

"Okay, okay!" said Izzy.

I smiled. "We are about to crack this case wide open."

12 | One Wild Ride!

Izzy and I ran into the fire station. Chief Vince was seated, talking with Nina.

"Hi, Hilde! Hi, Izzy!" Nina said, waving us over.

"Did you find Boots?" I asked.

"Not yet," Nina replied. "But I'm sure he'll come home soon. Right now, I'm trying to help with the fire investigation."

"Sorry, girls," said Chief Vince, "but I don't have any new information for you."

I grabbed the picture of Nina's Antique Store out of Izzy's hands and set it down in front of him.

"Well, *we* have some new information for *you*," I said, smiling.

"What's this?" he asked, picking up the picture.

"We took it last week, right after Nina hung up her new lights," said Izzy.

Chief Vince glanced at the picture, then looked up at us. "I'm not trying to be rude, girls, but I don't have time for this right now."

I held our magnifying glass over the right side of the roof in the picture.

"Do you have time for *that*?" I said, pointing at the zoomed-in area.

Chief Vince jumped up out of his seat so quickly it made Archie yelp. *Woof!*

"Oh, my!" he exclaimed. "There are birds' nests up against that light!"

"Hello?" said Izzy. "Will someone please fill me in on what is happening here?!"

"Me too!" said Nina, leaning in for a closer look.

"Go ahead, Hilde," said Chief Vince.

I turned to Izzy. "Remember when Georgie and Juliet were collecting small sticks and twigs as kindling — to help Dad start the fire?"

Izzy looked confused. "Yeah, but what does our cookout have to do with the fire at Nina's store?"

I playfully flicked Izzy in the ear. "Duh! What is a bird's nest made of?"

Izzy clapped her hands together. "Small sticks and twigs!" she exclaimed.

"Yes," I said. "And because these nests were wedged in the gutter between the wooden wall and Nina's new lights, the heat from the lights set one of the nests on fire."

"So it really wasn't Mrs. Brown's candles," said Izzy. "It was the nests!"

"That's right," agreed Chief Vince. "A bird's nest against a hot light is a fire hazard."

I wrote that down. It sounded like a great quote for my story.

Nina jumped out of her seat. "Mrs. Brown is about to miss the Pet Prowl because she thinks *she* caused the fire!" she said. "We need to tell her right away!"

I looked at my phone. It was 1:45 p.m. The Pet Prowl was supposed to begin in fifteen minutes.

"We'll never get there and back in time," I said. "If Mrs. Brown isn't on Market Street at two to register everyone, they'll cancel the parade!"

"That's not going to happen!" said Chief Vince. "Follow me!"

He rushed into the garage and climbed into the fire truck. Nina got in the passenger seat. Archie jumped up on her lap.

"Climb in the back, girls," he said. "I'll get us to Mrs. Brown's house in no time!"

13 Crack in the Door

Chief Vince sped up Mill Street. Izzy and I held on tight. This was our first time in a fire truck. We couldn't stop smiling!

The chief took a sharp left on Eighth Street.

The fire truck stopped in front of Mrs. Brown's house.

Izzy and I jumped out and ran to the door. We both knocked loudly.

After a few seconds, a voice called through the door. "Hello?"

"Mrs. Brown! It's Hilde and Izzy," I said. "There's something we *HAVE* to tell you!"

"I'm sorry, girls, but I'm in no shape for visitors," Mrs. Brown said through the door.

"But the fire wasn't your fault! Your candles didn't start the fire. It was a bird's nest!" I yelled.

The door opened a crack. Mrs. Brown's eyes were red and puffy. I could tell she had been crying.

"Birds can't start fires, girls," she said. "I appreciate you trying to make me feel better, but I think you should go."

Mrs. Brown began to shut the door.

Just then, Chief Vince stepped forward. "These girls are telling the truth," he said. "The fire started on the right-hand side of the building's roof. There's a picture that shows bird nests in the same spot — and they're pressed against Nina's outdoor lights."

The door opened wider.

"So I didn't cause the fire?" Mrs. Brown asked.

"No, it was just an accident," said Nina, stepping forward. "*I* should've checked my gutters before hanging up those hot lights."

"Mrs. Brown, we need to hurry," I said. "The Pet Prowl is about to start, and it can't start without you!"

"Well, then," Mrs. Brown said, taking a deep breath. She grabbed her special Pet Prowl binder. "I guess we have a parade to get to!"

Izzy and I cheered!

The five of us rushed to the fire truck. This time Mrs. Brown squeezed up front with Chief Vince and Nina. Archie jumped in the back with Izzy and me.

"Hold on tight!" shouted Chief Vince.

The fire truck sped away with the sirens blaring. We reached Market Street in a flash!

Pets were lined up in adorable costumes.

Mrs. Brown started setting up her registration table.

While she registered pets, I explained to the crowd what *really* caused the fire at Nina's Antique Store.

After I finished speaking, everyone's eyes moved to Mrs. Brown.

"Oh! What a relief!" exclaimed Sue, placing her hand to her heart.

Then the mayor stepped up to the microphone. "Pets of Selinsgrove," he announced. "Get ready to prowl!"

14 A Surprise from Above

Pets and their owners began parading down Market Street.

I sat down to watch the parade. Izzy took pictures of all the pets.

I saw Nina standing off to the side. *It's too bad Boots didn't come back in time for the parade.*

"Look at Zeus and Brian," said Izzy. "They look so cute!"

Zeus let out a happy bark. "Ruff! Ruff!"

Then I heard a strange voice, screeching, "Ruff! Ruff!"

It sounded sort of like Zeus, but it was coming from above.

Everyone looked up. There were three birds in the sky. One of them was Boots!

"Ruff! Ruff!" He was repeating the bark he had just heard from Zeus.

Boots still had ashy black spots all over. And there were two ash-covered birds with him.

"The blue jays!" I cried out.

"Those must be the baby chicks' parents!" exclaimed Izzy.

I laughed. *"That's* why Boots was rooting through the ashes at Nina's store. He was looking for his friends!"

Just then, Boots swooped down and landed on Nina's shoulder.

"Boots! I missed you so much!" she said. She gave him kisses on his beak!

Then the blue jays swooped down and landed on the bird feeder.

Officer Pam rushed over to the blue jays. "I know two little chicks who are going to be happy to see you both!" she said.

Izzy and I clapped.

Mayor Jeff walked up to the microphone. "It's time to announce the winner of today's Pet Prowl! Would our judge please come up?"

Officer Pam stepped up to the microphone.

"That parakeet's Dalmatian costume is the most fantastic Pet Prowl costume Selinsgrove has ever seen!" she said, pointing to Boots.

"We have a winner!" said Mayor Jeff. "The one-thousand-dollar prize for this year's Pet Prowl goes to Nina and her parakeet, Boots!"

"Boots really *does* look like a Dalmatian," I said to Izzy.

Nina was smiling from ear to ear. "Thank you!" she said. "This money will help me rebuild my store!"

Izzy and I high-fived.

"Time to type up my story," I said, taking out my laptop. I turned to Izzy. "And I can't wait to see your pictures!"

Just then, a bright flash streaked across the sky! "What was that?" asked Izzy.

"I don't know," I said. "But I have a feeling our next story might be out of this world!"

Exclusive!

FIRE! FIRE!

BY HILDE KATE LYSIAK

Nina's Antique Store was destroyed by a fire! [2]

PHOTO CREDIT: ISABEL ROSE LYSIAK

A bird's nest started the fire at 9 a.m. No one was hurt, but the store was destroyed. The heat from owl-shaped lights that Nina had hung on the outside of the store ignited three blue jay nests. The small sticks and twigs from the nests set the roof on fire, which quickly spread to the rest of the wooden building. [3]